A Yogi

and his

Corvette

An Inspirational Story About Love and Growth

by

M. H. Curtis

ISBN: 978-1-7337992-8-7

Cover art: M. H. Curtis

Dedicated to A Divine True Friend

and to

Gagandeep Singh

Acknowledgements

There are so many people to thank for this work... Gagan for storyline input, other shy people providing editorial help, and of course the many people who have been inspirations for various parts of the story. I would also like to thank the enlightened beings who help us on our way, help us to grow, help us to move forward, and the Infinite One who guides us and allows us to create opportunities for growth and understanding when that is what we seek! And last but not least, a big thanks goes out to you the reader, may you derive some benefit and enjoyment from this story...

M. H. Curtis

Contents

EARLY YEARS OF MIKEY

Mikey, whose given name was Michael, grew up in a modest family environment. People were very fond of the young boy, and he was often called Mikey by his parents and friends. As a child Mikey displayed an unusual devotion to and love for God. At the time of Mikey's youth, the highest living incarnation of God was believed to be a Yogi whose abode was in the remote regions of the Himalaya Mountains, and who had been called by many names but in recent years was simply referred to as Baba.

While growing up, although given many toys, Mikey was never strongly attached to them and when friends came over to play with him, if he noticed that a friend was fond of a particular toy he would happily give the toy to the friend. This generosity caused some commotion in the household because his parents worked hard to provide things for Mikey, and one day they told him that he should not give away his toys. He respectfully listened to the instructions of his parents, and when they finished, he asked his parents if sharing was God's way, and if attachment to anything meant being anchored in the material world. His parents could not dispute his point for they were also very devoted people and knew the injunctions of their religion which frowned upon material attachment.

Meditating upon the issue one evening, his father had a revelation about the toys and about Mikey's willingness to let them go so easily. The next day Mikey's father approached him to have a talk. "Mikey", he said.

"Yes father" Mikey answered.

His father continued, "I want to ask you what you believe the purpose of your toys are?"

Mikey replied, "of course father, my toys are for entertaining me and to share with my friends."

"Yes", agreed his father who continued, "but do you realize there is another important reason that you have toys?"

Mikey replied, "no father, please tell me what that important reason is."

"It is so that you have tools with which to help you learn about and experience life. Some of your toys challenge you, some are simply for entertainment which helps you achieve inner reflection, and some are for you to share, to learn the transitory nature of everything. Do you understand?" His father asked.

"Yes father, my toys are tools to help me grow," was Mikey's response.

Mikey's father smiled knowing that his son was learning a valuable lesson and also hoping his son now realized the value of the toys he was given.

When his friends came over to play with him, Mikey continued to give his toys to friends who seemed particularly attached to them. His father became concerned and decided to have another talk with Mikey. His father asked, "Mikey, didn't we discover that your toys are tools to help you grow in a variety of ways?"

"Yes father" came Mikey's response.

"Why then do you continue to give your toys to your friends?" His father asked.

Mikey replied, "father, it is because my friends do not have some of the tools I have, so it seemed important to share my tools with them."

His father considered what Mikey had said and nodding his head in understanding left Mikey to himself.

FINDING A GURU

So it was as Mikey grew...he was wise beyond his years and the material world did not prevent him from retaining his spiritual devotion. In fact, if anything Mikey seemed to view the material world as an anchor slowing and even preventing spiritual growth, and he had even rejected a few toys he had been given when he was younger.

As Mikey approached the age of 12 years, his parents decided that it

would be best to find a Guru for him.
They made this decision because of his
giving and loving nature, and his
constant engaging in meditation and
inner reflection. They felt it was the
right course, really the only course for
his life. This was not a decision made
lightly because it meant that once Mikey
was with a guru in an ashram, they may
not see their son again for a very long
time, possibly not for many years.

While searching for a guru, and
during what his parents felt may be his

last year in school while living in their home, Mikey was provided a tutor for his subject in the sciences. It turned out, unbeknownst to his parents, that the tutor was a very spiritual man and flamed the fire of spirituality in Mikey's heart. His tutor happened to be a disciple of Baba, the yogi in the mountains, and having spent a significant amount of time with him eventually his tutor had become one with the Infinite, a fully self-realized yogi. Being such a person, he recognized the spiritual devotion of

Mikey, and though knowing he was not Mikey's guru, the tutor still helped Mikey open his mind to more fully explore the amazing spiritual world, along with the true nature of life which is bliss, and love for the Provider of all things.

Eventually a guru was found whose ashram was located very far from the home of Mikey and his parents. Mikey's parents planned a trip to visit the guru with Mikey, and decided to take the personal belongings Mikey would need in the event the decision was made for him to stay.

When the time came Mikey and his parents travelled to the guru's ashram, a journey which took more than half a day of driving. Upon arriving the guru had a welcoming smile, but it was recognized by Mikey's parents that the guru was a stern man, a strict disciplinarian. Mikey's parents believed such firmness in a guru would help Mikey balance his continual sharing and loving nature with a more realistic and disciplined approach to the things in life. The guru could see the hope of Mikey's parents and assured them that they had nothing to fear, that his approach of molding young disciples through righteousness had been successful for many years and that he was confident the techniques would be successful in helping Mikey.

Mikey's parents embraced their young man-child and felt comfortable that Mikey would be in good care with this guru who had a very confident approach, even though it seemed a little unmalleable. His parents left and they cried on the way home knowing how much they would miss their son. Mikey too was a bit more torn about the separation from his parents than he felt he would be. The guru recognized the reaction and knew it was best to let it work itself out.

As weeks passed at the ashram, Mikey worked to fulfill the expectations of his guru. The guru typically guided his disciples by pointing out their flaws, and providing corrective guidance to their thoughts through which the disciples understood and pursued the correct line of thinking. The guru's approach in changing thought translated into the correct action, a manifestation of correct thought.

Though the guru watched Mikey carefully and spent time focusing on the inner being of Mikey, he found it difficult to correct any of Mikey's actions and consequently thought processes. Because Mikey was such a loving person the only flaw which seemed apparent was that he was too loving...which of course was not a flaw at all.

This loving personality characteristic the guru saw in Mikey was somewhat foreign to him and so he continued keeping a close observance of his newest disciple. One issue the guru eventually realized was that the other disciples were being influenced by Mikey's love, which seemed to provide a change in them. The guru recognized that they, the other disciples, were becoming more loving themselves and as such were not as dedicated to correcting their inner flaws as they were in expressing a loving attitude in all of their activities. This meant the disciples were getting along better with each other because they were more accepting of each other, but the guru saw this as a setback reflecting less devotion to the "inner work" he had identified individually for them. The guru was immersed in a righteous approach to finding God, whereas Mikey's natural disposition was a loving approach, and the guru felt this was adversely impacting the other disciples.

Mikey had no issues with the regimentation of the guru, but the guru continually tried to suppress the love Mikey expressed toward all because of the impact it had on the other disciples, and the effect it was having on the guru's approach to disciple training. As a result, a continual conflict, almost a tug of war, so to speak, developed between the guru and Mikey. Because of his loving approach Mikey did not recognize it, but for the guru it became a constant challenge to train the disciples through his rigid approach. It was for that reason alone the guru decided that having Mikey at the ashram was a poor fit.

As it turned out, after Mikey had been at the ashram for only a couple of months the guru contacted Mikey's parents and told them he was not a good fit for the group and they needed to come and get him. At this news his parents were shocked, wondering what could have happened to create this wedge between the guru and Mikey.

Mikey's parents immediately planned and made the trip to go and get Mikey and bring him home so they could assess what happened with their son. When they arrived at the ashram, all was quiet. The guru was seated with all of the young students around him including Mikey. There was no sign or feeling of any friction between the guru and Mikey. In fact, all they felt was a deep sense of love the young disciples had for the guru. This was puzzling to them.

When Mikey saw his parents he asked his guru, in a most gracious way, if he could be dismissed. The guru nodded in approval but said nothing, nor did he look up at Mikey or his parents. Mikey got up and smiled at his parents and they followed him to his room where his things were gathered in a bundle which Mikey picked up. Then Mikey knelt down and prayed, "oh

Heavenly Father and Divine Mother,
thank thee for all of thy gifts of love.
Not only the love you bestow upon me
daily, but the love you also bestow upon
the guru."

Mikey got up and they left the
ashram for the long journey home. On
the way his parents asked what
happened, why the guru said that having
Mikey at the ashram was not working
out. Mikey told his parents that the guru
was often very stern, and so one day
Mikey decided to pray to God to put

love in the heart of the guru as He had put love in his own heart. Mikey said that God listened to his request and answered it. The next day the guru found it impossible to continue with his training by any means other than love. The guru became quite disoriented and spent an entire day meditating about it. Within a week the guru told Mikey that he would have to leave because he, the guru, was not familiar with any means of converting disciples except with righteousness, which had always been his way. With Mikey at his ashram, he could not continue helping the other disciples on their righteous path to inner freedom.

When Mikey finished the explanation, his parents did not know what to say except that they would immediately begin the search for another guru and were glad to have him come back home until another ashram was found. Then his parents looked at each other and realized their son was a young Man-of-God already, and that he must be very special in the Eyes of God.

FINDING THE RIGHT GURU

Through some friends Mikey's parents heard about a guru living near them, less than an hour's drive from their home. They also learned that this guru was very selective about taking on new disciples, but if accepted a disciple was almost assured success on the spiritual path in life. This time Mikey's parents contacted the guru and made an appointment to meet with him, without the accompaniment of their son. On the day of the appointment, they travelled to see this guru without Mikey so that they could focus on meeting and developing an understanding about him, and the approach he used with his disciples.

When Mikey's parents arrived at the ashram, they saw no sign of welcome which made them feel a bit odd. They approached the door to the ashram and knocked. A disciple opened the door and smiling at them he motioned them to follow him as he led them into the home which served as the ashram. In the parlor they found the guru sitting in the middle of the room with the disciples surrounding him. The guru, upon seeing Mikey's parents, got up to greet them and before they could speak, he said, "welcome, you are the parents of a child for whom you seek a guru and you called to come and meet with me. The first guru you found for your son, whom you lovingly refer to as Mikey, did not work out because he maintained a more regimented path than the natural loving approach your son has. This ashram is a perfect fit for

Mikey and I am pleased you decided to 'take a chance' to come visit me."

At this both of his parents were somewhat shocked because they had not mentioned any of this to the guru when they made the appointment. As they were looking at each other, the guru smiled and told them not to worry, they had made a good decision. Then he asked if they would like some tea and perhaps a tour of the ashram. They declined the offer of tea but readily accepted the invitation to see the ashram. They were shown the garden area where the disciples grew food and learned about loving and caring for the plants they nurtured, and learned how mother earth can provide many of the necessities of life. They were shown the library with books for the disciples to study. They were also shown some bedrooms, a kitchen, the laundry facilities, and a number of other amenities of the ashram. One of the bedrooms they were shown was to be for Mikey, at the times he would be staying there. At this they asked what the guru meant. The guru told them that because they lived relatively close, he would encourage Mikey to spend time with them so that he would maintain a familiarity with life outside of the ashram, and also so that he might enjoy the love of his family when time permitted it. Mikey's parents smiled in pleasant surprise because this was not expected, but it was a condition they gladly embraced.

After discussions with the guru, it was decided that his parents would bring

Mikey to the ashram to meet the guru the following Sunday afternoon. They would also bring clothing and personal items for Mikey in the event he was comfortable in staying, in which case he could begin his discipleship immediately.

When his parents arrived home, they told Mikey about the guru and his kindness, and also about his awareness of the situation with the other guru. They told him they believed this was the "fit" they were looking for in a guru for

Mikey. Mikey smiled as he listened to
them and then asked if he could go to
meditate for a while. After a short
meditation Mikey rejoined his parents
and told them he was looking forward to
meeting his new guru and was happy
that the ashram was not too far away.

The following Sunday Mikey and
his parents arrived at the ashram and this
time the guru was waiting to greet them.
This guru was a kind and loving man
and Mikey was instantly drawn to him
and his obvious loving approach with

his disciples. In fact, Mikey seemed to recognize him from dreams he had years ago when he was younger. The guru also recognized Mikey and was pleased that his new disciple, a loving manifestation of God, was now with him so he could help Mikey free his mind of the dross necessary to achieve the final goal on the spiritual path.

His parents left Mikey with the guru at the ashram and the guru spent the day familiarizing Mikey with the facilities. The guru gave Mikey some responsibilities but told him not to be too concerned with a schedule. During his first few weeks at the ashram Mikey spent much of his time with his guru, but with the encouragement of his guru he decided he would spend time with his family as well.

At first Mikey only wanted to stay with his guru but his guru told him that even those on the path of the yogi must also understand the non-yogi way that most people choose in life, and all of the consequences of that other path. The guru told Mikey it would be important for him to have that understanding later in his life of helping others. Mikey was not sure what the guru meant, but accepted what he was told with all of the joy that he seemed to accept everything in life.

The first time he returned home from the ashram Mikey told his parents that although he stayed at the ashram of the guru, he also wanted to spend some time at home. His parents welcomed the idea and were very pleased about

Mikey's decision. Mikey also continued to go to the school he had been attending before finding a guru. It turned out that Mikey's life hadn't seemed to change much. He still went to school, he spent some time at home, and he found a lot of time to spend with his Guru who gradually continued to open his awareness to the spiritual side of life, to the Infinite within him. The guru showed him how to allow that Infinite part of him guide him in most every way, and as this process progressed

Mikey became even more reflective of the loving ways of God.

As Mikey spent time at home, he also became more aware of the life driven by the material world. Part of this education was observing the ways of his parents who were very loving people themselves, and yet he saw how they had many things in life to deal with. Mikey's father worked and during the week would leave home daily to go to his job. His mother stayed home taking care of the household duties and also went to the market to buy food and other household necessities. Mikey also noted around the end of every month his parents discussed their finances and paid monthly bills for their home and utilities, and for other services they received.

Sometimes Mikey heard his parents disagree about their finances, his mother wanted to give more to charity and other relatives, and his father wanted to put more away for unexpected emergencies, for "a rainy day." Mikey was very pleased to be spending more time with his parents and to have the opportunity to gain an understanding of the challenges in life. He also saw that though his parents had the challenges of others, their challenges related to helping others in need, and were not due to wanting more for themselves. Mikey recognized this to be different than the struggles of so many other families he had witnessed, primarily the families of his friends from school, who seemed to always struggle to get more.

With every new opportunity suggested by his guru, Mikey understood that his guru was conditioning him for his adult life by providing training for the challenges he must someday face. The lessons made him feel even closer to his guru who, through love and a soft approach, opened more doors of expression for the love already abundant in Mikey's heart and mind.

MIKEY'S PERSONAL CHALLENGE

As days and months went by at the ashram, Mikey developed a personal issue which he kept hidden deeply within himself. He had never experienced jealousy or insecurity before, but felt like it had slowly crept into his life. His guru expressed love so easily for all the disciples that sometimes Mikey felt a bit lost, especially when other disciples seemed to receive so much more love from their guru than he. Mikey struggled with his feelings for a long time and did not share them with anyone, nor did he let them affect the way he responded to others. Fortunately for Mikey, his guru was fully self-realized and became aware of the issue Mikey was dealing with.

In an attempt to help Mikey deal with the insecurity, one day his guru asked Mikey if there were any issues bothering him, or anything he would like to talk about. Mikey looked at his guru and got the feeling he knew about Mikey's developing insecurity, and yet he did not feel that it was the right time to discuss the issue, and he also felt a little embarrassed about it, so he told his guru that he did not want to discuss any issues with him at the moment. This response enabled him to be completely honest and at the same time avoid having to openly reveal the issue he had tried so hard to deal with. His guru smiled with understanding and told Mikey perhaps another time would be more appropriate.

One day, not long after the guru asked Mikey if there were any issues bothering him, his guru called Mikey to join him in the garden. There the guru was tending the plants. Some plants were flourishing and some were not. The guru pointed out to Mikey that the flourishing plants looked so healthy, so wonderful, that they did not need the same amount of love and attention as the plants that were not doing well. The guru explained it was the same with disciples. Some like Mikey were so full of love they did not require the outward expression of love and attention, but others whose lives had been more challenging, needed to be shown love continually and in that way, they were molded to be ever reflective of the Love of the Divine Creator. Mikey considered what his guru had told him and smiled, having had his insecurity instantly resolved with the simple explanation from his guru. Mikey thanked his guru and asked if he could remain and help tend the plants that needed it. His guru smiled back at him and said, "of course for together we will always be helping nurture plants and people in this garden of life."

THE UNIQUE FAMILY OF A DISCIPLE

One day at the ashram the guru, while meditating on the lives of various disciples, became aware that one disciple's life was about to take a strange turn in the already sad and complex family of the disciple. The father of that particular disciple had been involved with corruption and graft for many years. He also enforced his business relationships by occasionally using extreme measures, much to the regret of

48

the recipients of the strong-arm tactics. What the Guru had seen through his meditation was, due to the severe conduct of the disciple's father, his father's life would end soon. The guru also saw that the family members who had benefitted from the malfeasance of the father would also suffer from the bad karma. The guru became concerned about the disciple and the impact of the upcoming karmic justice on his family. The guru talked with the disciple and explained that there would be some upcoming unfortunate events for his family, and the guru felt the disciple would benefit the most by remaining at the ashram, even if his family tried to take him home. The disciple understood and promised to meditate about the situation.

Within a few days the family members of the disciple, including his mother and an aunt, along with a sister and brother, showed up to see him. His mother told the disciple his father had died, and asked him to come home for a little while. The disciple asked his mother and other family members if he could have a day to consider the situation. The disciple had been at the ashram for several years and because his family had rarely visited him, he did not know much about the business his father had been engaged in, nor did his family members have any idea about his life at the ashram. The family agreed and told him they would return the following afternoon.

In meditating about the circumstances of his family, the disciple became aware that his family had no intention of allowing him to come back to the ashram. The family members returned the next day. The disciple asked his family what would happen if he did not go home with them. He was told that he would be disowned as a family member never to be allowed to return to them again. He asked for a few minutes to speak to his guru, then realized that if he did take time to speak with his guru and then declined to go, they would blame the guru. So instead, he stayed and told his family that he did not believe they had any intention of allowing him to return. He also told them he would come home when he was ready and if they were truly his family, they would accept him whenever that happened to be. He then asked them to leave.

These particular circumstances had a profound impact on Mikey because Mikey had developed a close friendship with the disciple, and became aware of the disciple's family problems through their guru. Due to his guru's alerting him to the disciple's issue, Mikey also meditated about the circumstances of the disciple and his family. From his meditation Mikey developed a significant understanding of what was happening to his disciple friend, and had never encountered such an outward expression of manipulation his friend was experiencing by his family. He also could see the influence of his guru on the disciple, and the disciple's ability to gain intuition about the situation that others might not have. These life circumstances reinforced Mikey's belief that spiritual pursuit was the best path in life, and developing a relationship with God was important for everyone.

THE DISCIPLE OF
QUESTIONABLE CHARACTER

There were new disciples who came occasionally, and once in a while some left. On one occasion when a new disciple came, Mikey received a lesson about the nature of people and how it is often hidden behind a smile and seemingly friendly demeanor.

The new disciple in question had joined the ashram and was friendly to everyone. He had a warm smile and was quick to agree with people and listen patiently to their stories. As with all the new disciples, the guru attuned to this new disciple with techniques that allowed him to see a deeper character of the individual. What he saw was a bit of a surprise in that the inner character did not coincide with the outer friendly person.

The guru assigned the new disciple, whose name was David, the after-dinner clean-up duties. It was also part of this duty to deliver desserts to the disciples after dinner. Because of the inner nature the guru had seen, he was certain that David would take advantage of his opportunity to help himself with more than his portion of dessert, because one of his flaws was greed and another was over-eating. For a couple of days David performed his task without hidden motives, but on the third day a most amazing dessert had been prepared for the disciples, a chocolate mousse made in individual serving dishes for the disciples. This was something that David could not resist. While David was busy in the kitchen, because it was his night to clean up after the meal, one of the other disciples was asked to help David serve the desserts. This request occurred while David was out of the dining room, and David was quite surprised to see the disciple walk into the kitchen only to find David eating one of the mousse desserts rather than cleaning up the dinner dishes.

The other disciple turned around and walked out. Almost immediately all of the disciples re-entered the kitchen to watch David. Interestingly, no one said anything, but the disciple who was asked to help went to the refrigerator to get the desserts for the other disciples. He noticed that it did not appear there were enough desserts for everyone. Looking around he saw two additional dirty mousse dishes in the sink. The disciple turned to David and asked, "did you eat the two mousse desserts from those dishes in the sink?"

David turned very red and started to lie, yet knew it was to no avail. From then on none of the other disciples went out of their way to associate with David, and before long the rejection was more than he could bear and he left the ashram to return to his old ways, leading to a challenging and painful life.

Even though the treatment of David seemed contrary to the foundation of the ashram, the other disciples also learned that the inclinations of someone like David's should not be encouraged nor tolerated, which is why they avoided him. Had David been sincere with an apology, along with a commitment to make an effort to change his ways, all of the disciples would have helped him grow. Sadly, it was not in David to apologize for his shortcomings nor have regret about his greed.

THE SELF-CENTERED
DISCIPLE WHO CHANGED

Another situation occurred at the
ashram that dealt with a disciple named
Geoffrey, who happened to have a
challenging personality, and was a bit
egocentric. Mikey along with all of the
other disciples tolerated Geoffrey's self-
centeredness, partly from the training in
the ashram, and partly due to the
foundation of showing love for all. This
basic foundation was to practice
patience and tolerance for all, even other

disciples who had not yet fully absorbed the lessons of the ashram into their own character.

One day the parents of Geoffrey made a surprise visit to the ashram to see their son. They were taken aback when shown to some chairs in a waiting area, able to observe the disciples sitting around the guru listening to a discussion about some key points in the Bhagavad Gita, but receiving no formal greeting. When Geoffrey saw his parents, he immediately got up to greet them without even requesting permission to do so from the guru. The guru smiled inwardly at this behavior, having already recognized the self-indulgent traits in Geoffrey.

After greeting his parents, Geoffrey stood waiting to be acknowledged by the guru, for he wanted the guru to join his parents and give them the attention Geoffrey believed they were entitled to. The guru however ignored both Geoffrey and his parents, and continued with his dissertation about the Gita. Normally, if the guru knew of a visit by the parents of a disciple ahead of time, the parents would be immediately welcomed and given due respect, but on this occasion the parents of Geoffrey did not provide any advanced notice of their visit. It was because of the lack of advance notice that the guru continued with his discourse until it was finished for the day, as if no visitors had arrived. It was another 45 minutes that Geoffrey's parents had to wait before being greeted by the guru.

Of course, Geoffrey was not happy about this treatment and intended to share his displeasure with the guru, yet when the discussion was finished the guru got up and with a genuine smile and inner warmth greeted Geoffrey's parents. The parents stood up not knowing what to say because they recognized that the guru was sincere, and they knew of course that they arrived without notice. Finally, the father of Geoffrey apologized for the interruption. Then the guru also apologized for not being able to acknowledge Geoffrey's parents immediately, and explained that the disciples were his number one priority, and the lessons he provided them from time to time helped them with their spiritual growth and progress. Geoffrey's parents said they understood and were happy to have waited and then have the opportunity to meet with the guru.

The guru recognized Geoffrey's feelings and inwardly knew it was an

important lesson he was learning.
Geoffrey was a bit confused because his
parents had always provided him
whatever he said he needed, and yet his
parents were now outwardly
acknowledging the needs of the others.
While Geoffrey was going through his
inner turmoil, the guru offered tea to his
parents, and engaged them in
conversation letting them know the
ashram was running very smoothly, and
the disciples were progressing on their
spiritual paths. The guru did not talk
specifically about Geoffrey nor did

Geoffrey's parents ask about his progress. This also was a bit of a blow to Geoffrey because he wanted his parents to be proud of his progress, so this became something else for him to consider.

Geoffrey's parents eventually left the ashram after a very nice visit with the guru. After his parents left the ashram, Geoffrey approached the guru and thanked him for the hospitality he showed his parents. The guru, aware of Geoffrey's inner confusion, asked him if there was anything else on his mind concerning the visit. Geoffrey said there was but he would rather not discuss it at that moment, that he needed to consider it for a while if that was ok with the guru, to which the guru smiled and said "yes". Then the guru said to Geoffrey, "we are all in this together, dependent on each other and not just ourselves. If this was not true, I would not have had a loving guru to provide me training, nor would I be here providing training for you and the other disciples. Because of this truth we must always consider others whom we find with us on our paths, and show them the respect and consideration that we would like them to show us."

Geoffrey immediately understood the truth in the guru's words, and they had such a profound effect on him that he changed and abandoned his self-centered ways. Geoffrey learned a big lesson on his spiritual path that day, and it helped him look at his whole life differently from that point on. Eventually Geoffrey left the ashram and became a teacher. His teaching position was in a school with many students of his own to teach and guide along their way in life. The lesson he learned about not being selfish was the key he needed to open his mind to spiritual progress and succeed on his path as a teacher helping others.

MIKEY'S LIFE AT THE ASHRAM

As Mikey's stay at the ashram continued, it was obvious that his loving approach had a profound effect on all of the disciples. Many of the disciples sought out Mikey's help with personal issues when the guru was occupied or in deep meditation. Mikey's willingness to help the other disciples never went unnoticed by his guru, who had always been very fond of Mikey, and of the special gift of love he had.

Often when disciples had bad news from home or were saddened about being away from home and missing their loved ones, it was Mikey who they turned to for consoling. Mikey's approach to problems and issues made the disciples feel special, and that the world revolved around love. It was easy for Mikey to open up their hearts allowing them to see the Infinite Love within themselves.

Normally in an ashram it would be the guru's place to provide such comfort, yet because of Mikey's gift, and the process of preparing him for his future, the guru was happy to allow him to provide comfort to the other disciples when they needed it. The guru knew that Mikey could truly help all of them spiritually, as well as in the physical world.

Over the years, the guru had spent a bit of time meditating about Mikey and gained some clear insight about the course of Mikey's life and how to best prepare him for it. When Mikey was approaching the completion of his required education, the guru suggested that Mikey continue with his education so that he had a college degree when he became a guru, which would provide him with more credibility. Mikey heard his guru mention that he would be a guru and wondered about it, but soon forgot the comment as he followed his guru's suggestion and prepared to enter college.

MIKEY GOES TO COLLEGE

While Mikey was finishing his pre-college education he enrolled in a social science program at a local four-year college. Mikey began his coursework in the college program immediately following the completion of his required education. As time passed at college some of his fellow students became aware of Mikey's devotion to God. Mikey occasionally brought a few of the students, those who seemed to have a devotional nature, to the ashram and introduced them to his

guru. Of the few students he brought to

the ashram once in a while one showed

enough interest and sincerity to actually

receive discipleship from his guru, while

others were advised to stay on their path.

One college friend of Mikey's who

asked the guru about his path was

actually told that he would have a family

and one of his children would follow the

spiritual path. Many students were

positively influenced by Mikey even

though he seemed more interested in

following God than providing attention to his studies.

One professor of Mikey's was a non-believer, and continually tried to elevate himself by lowering Mikey through criticism and a demeaning candor towards him. The guru, aware of the issue the professor had with Mikey, or perhaps more accurately the issue Mikey had and yet accepted from his professor, made a point to approach the professor about the issue.

One day at a market the professor was shopping and not aware that the holy person who approached him was Mikey's guru. The guru engaged the professor in a conversation and the professor happily obliged and proudly told the guru that he was a college professor. The guru smiled and asked him what his purpose was as a professor. The professor said it was to educate students. The guru asked if the professor knew all there was to know about education and its application. The professor thoughtfully and reluctantly answered no. Then the guru asked him why it was necessary to belittle in public those who followed a different path than himself. The professor said it wasn't. The guru then told the professor that Mikey was his disciple. The professor was quite surprised and blushed. Then the professor, stripped of his ego, apologized and told the guru it would not happen again.

Mikey's college years sailed by for him, almost as a dream. During his time in college, he established a pattern of providing minimal attention to his assignments, attempting just enough work to achieve passing scores. This enabled him to spend more time with his guru, and he even found quality time to spend with his family. Mikey's parents were surprised that the decision was made for Mikey to attend college, and were delighted that even with college work he was able to spend some time with them. Of course, Mikey's most important goal continued to be spending time with his guru, which he did on a regular basis. His guru was pleased with his progress in college as well as his spiritual progress.

In 4 years, Mikey graduated from college. After college he decided to stay at the ashram on a full-time basis in order to spend more time with his guru, to which his guru did not object. Mikey still continued to visit his parents often, and life for Mikey didn't feel like it could be much better.

MIKEY BECOMES A MONK

A few months after graduating from college, Mikey's guru approached him one day and told him on the following morning he would be initiated with the formal rites of acceptance as a monk, if Mikey was still willing to become a monk. Mikey was elated and hugged his guru and thanked him, because becoming a monk had been the stated goal of his life.

The following morning Mikey put on a clean robe and presented himself to his guru. His guru smiled at his loving disciple and handed Mikey a new robe, a robe that had been died the ochre color of monks robes, and was made of silk. Mikey bowed in gratitude and accepted the robe, taking it to his room to put on for the ceremony. Mikey returned donning his new robe, and his guru asked him to sit before the alter. Eight candles were placed on the alter, and as the guru lit each candle, he said powerful words of blessing to Mikey, and pausing after each candle lighting, asked Mikey to meditate on the words which were being spoken to him. The words were to guide Mikey's inner being and also help open his spiritual awareness. When the guru finished the candle lighting ceremony, he asked Mikey to stand and welcomed him as a monk.

Normally when a disciple became a monk, he would be involved in choosing his own name, but on this occasion Mikey's guru told Mikey that

his name would be Dveshananda.
Mikey was bewildered about the name,
knowing that "ananda" meant bliss and
divine love, but Mikey was not familiar
with "dvesh" and made a point to inquire
about its meaning. When he felt the
time was right, Mikey asked his guru
about the meaning of dvesh, and his
guru told him that it would be significant
to him later in his life, and for now he
should focus on the bliss and love part
of his name, which had been part of his
very being since the time of his birth.

Mikey accepted the words of his guru and accepted the name, though believed he would shorten it to simply "Ananda" if he ever had an ashram and disciples of his own. Mikey's guru also told him that though he was now a monk, he had always been a Yogi, or one who searched for God using a definitive method. His guru explained that not all yogis were monks, and not all monks were yogis.

Upon becoming a monk his guru had Mikey assume many of the duties and responsibilities of the ashram including; looking after the devotees, care and maintenance of the ashram, dealing with the local government officials, and other external affairs of the ashram.

Eventually, and to the surprise of everyone at the ashram, the government determined that the property of the ashram was needed for expansion, and proceedings began to acquire the property. One devotee was from a wealthy family with property in San

Diego, and the disciple obtained permission to donate some of the land to Mikey for construction of a new ashram.

The government eventually took possession of the existing ashram property and provided Mikey's guru with an amount of money, determined by the government, to be the fair value for the property. Mikey's guru decided to take the money and develop a small ashram in the mountains. A few of the guru's followers joined him to help build the new ashram. Many of the followers joined Mikey to help develop the property and begin a following in San Diego.

THE NEW ASHRAM AND CHURCH

Mikey with his new title Dveshananda, or as he and his followers referred to him "Ananda" for short, moved to San Diego with those disciples who chose to go with him. In the meantime, his guru retired to the location of where his new ashram would be built in the mountains with some disciples. Ananda had been told by his guru it was there he would spend the last portion of his life in solitude.

As the following of Ananda grew, progress was made to develop the land that had been donated to him. He and his disciples along with the new members, began the process of building and establishing a non-profit church and an ashram. A temporary church facility, with some bedrooms and a kitchen, was used for services and provided temporary living quarters to house many of the followers while the new facilities were being built. Donations poured into the organization, and progress to build the new church and ashram moved quickly. During this period Ananda felt a strong intuitive pull to visit his guru.

Ananda took a trip to see his guru in the new secluded mountain ashram his guru and disciples had built. Ananda felt so comfortable there with his guru that he stayed for a couple of months. Ananda wanted to stay longer, but his guru told him he had work to do helping others find their way on the path to the Infinite place of peace and love. His guru also told Ananda that they would not meet again while his guru had his current body, it was getting close to the time he must shed it, but he would always be with Ananda spiritually, and they would see each other again in the near future. Ananda found comfort in the assurances of his guru, they hugged and then Ananda departed, returning to San Diego to continue his mission to help others on the path toward their spiritual goal.

Upon his return, after his two-month absence to visit his guru, Ananda found that the church had been

completed by his very dedicated
disciples. He was pleased beyond
words, and very thankful to God, and the
motivation He had instilled in the
disciples to complete the beautiful
facility.

The following of Ananda
continued to grow, and the growth
occurred in a community where people
had a lot of money. Ananda and his
following continually helped people in
need, by feeding them, or providing
counsel, or letting people know that one

path may be better than another for them. Essentially, he gave them hope and love.

At one time during a particularly troubling period when a flu was affecting employers, and many people were being laid off due to restrictions imposed for safe distancing, the owner of a local kitchen, which made meals for the homeless, came to Ananda with an appeal of need for supplies, food, and workers to help continue to provide services to feed the needy and homeless.

Ananda rallied the disciples who, due to their extreme devotion to their guru and the ashram and their willingness to help the needy, donated the supplies and food that were necessary to continue to feed the hungry. Many of the disciples also volunteered when they could. The donations and labor provided by Ananda's disciples and followers enabled the food kitchen to continue its mission to help others in need.

Ananda, through his sermons and lessons, taught the disciples that the world was made through love, and that one of a persons highest objectives should be to exemplify love through every action, and toward every person. He taught that if someone did them wrong, the retribution for any wrongdoing belonged to God, and that when things in life did not go well or as planned, one should only look within themselves to attempt understanding, while avoiding affixing the blame on others, either in thought, speech, or deed. The disciples felt very comfortable with Ananda and his teachings, and because of this comfort their dedication to the spiritual path continued to grow and blossom.

One person, Will, who was a new follower and ambitious about becoming a disciple, was a salesman by profession had just started the process of learning about meditation and the spiritual path with lessons provided by Ananda. Will was so enthused about the lessons he believed that the lessons would meet with great success if they were distributed commercially. Will requested a meeting with Ananda to discuss his idea. At their meeting, Will, with the skill of a salesman, laid out a very thoughtful plan about the development and marketing of the lessons. Ananda listened to the presentation and paused for consideration after the conclusion of it. Ananda then asked Will what the purpose of the plan was. Will responded that he believed it would be commercially successful to mass-market the lessons. Ananda then asked, for what purpose. Will stated that there was a potential to make a lot of money from marketing the lessons. Ananda then asked, "do you believe that should be the purpose of the lessons?"

Will, thought about it briefly and replied, "it could be."

Ananda smiled and said to Will, "I see you are enthusiastic about this plan. Please continue to follow the lessons yourself. I would also ask that every evening before you go to sleep think about what God wants and who the lessons would best serve." Ananda then suggested that they meet again after the Sunday Sermon in one and a half weeks to revisit Will's plan. Ananda asked if that would work, and if Will was willing do what he asked him to.

Will listened intently to Ananda and promised to follow his instructions. Will told him he looked forward to their next meeting and excused himself.

A week and a half later Ananda and Will met again after the church sermon. As Ananda listened, Will told

him that he followed his instructions.

Will said that after 3 days of asking who

benefitted from the lessons, he was

overwhelmed by the feeling that there

were many people who were not on the

spiritual path, and that the lessons were

only for those who were willing to give

at least some dedication to the path and

the teaching of the lessons. Will

apologized for his presumption about

mass distribution of the lessons, and

more importantly he thanked Ananda for

his insight and loving approach in

helping Will understand. Ananda smiled and told Will he was happy that the lessons had been beneficial for him, and was glad to have discussed Will's idea.

UNEXPECTED GIFT

One follower, Richard, having
significant means, noticed that Ananda
drove an old car. This follower had
been very generous not only in
providing significant donations for the
construction of the new church and
ashram, but also in donating to the food
kitchen, and in many other ways.
Richard was also very devout in his
practice of the lessons and in attending
Sunday services, special services, and
social gatherings as well. The thing

about Richard was that his donations were always generous, as if the money meant nothing, and yet had that edge of, "we who belong to this organization and can afford the best" approach to all donations.

Ananda, in wanting to understand Richard and his motivation behind all of the donations, spent a bit of time meditating about Richard and the person inside the shell. Ananda discovered that Richard was a proud man, and also had some strong spiritual tendencies. In order to best deal with this Ananda developed the feeling to just let it play out, knowing that the need for more significant donations and the prideful giving, would eventually end.

To Ananda's surprise, in an attempt to not only provide him with a new car, but to show that the ashram was supported by generous disciples, Richard bought Ananda a new Corvette. Ananda received the car with surprise and concern. Within himself Ananda felt he did not want the car, and that having it sent the wrong message to his followers. Yet Ananda also recognized the genuine good-hearted nature of the gift and showed sincere appreciation to Richard for such a generous donation. Ananda took a ceremonious drive around the block in the new Corvette and then parked it. Ananda then spent time contemplating about how to deal with it, and worked to understand why it even came to him.

HIS GURU IS GONE

During the time of the receipt of, and confusion about the Corvette, Ananda received the shocking news that his guru was gone, had left his body, his earthly abode. At this news Ananda spent a couple of days meditating, searching for understanding, and for the consolation of the Infinite Provider of all.

Ananda traveled to the service for his guru at the small ashram his guru had established in the mountains, and planned to return to his own ashram after ensuring that the remaining disciples of his guru were established in such a way that would allow them to go continue their own following at the ashram. He also extended an offer to any of the disciples to join his ashram if they chose, that they would always be welcome.

The next day as he packed his bags to return to his ashram, and while Ananda found himself reflecting on his guru, a bright light appeared in his room and there before him his guru manifested in bodily form. Ananda embraced his guru as tears of joy rolled down his face. His guru smiled at Ananda the way he always did in the past to let Ananda know all would be ok. His guru told Ananda that he was now and forever more, a spiritual being and that as such he would always be helping to guide Ananda toward the Infinite goal. He also provided some additional techniques to Ananda which would allow him to easily access the spiritual

world while still on the physical plane.
These techniques would provide Ananda
a deeper understanding relating to the
needs of disciples. His guru also hinted
that he would see him again relatively
soon. Ananda was comforted by the
visit, and by the actual experience of
knowing that the life and death cycle
could be overcome.

After Ananda returned to his
ashram from the service of his guru, he
held a service for his guru with his own
following in the church. At the service

he talked about the love his guru showed him, and how his guru was the key which unlocked the answers to the questions of life, why we are here and what our purpose is. He also talked about the value of the love his guru showed not only him, but all of the many disciples his guru had taken "under his wing."

The followers were very moved by the service and many of them formed a committee to enhance the ashram by establishing a monument for Ananda's guru.

About this time, after the car had been parked for a while, it was discovered one day that it was missing, it had been stolen. Ananda felt responsible for the loss, but was relieved to no longer have the car to be concerned with, nor have it send the wrong message to the followers any more.

Eventually the police found the car, or at least parts of it, which provided the indication it had been parted out at a chop shop. Because the car was essentially found, and due to some quirk in the insurance policy because it was so new, the car ended up being replaced rather than providing a cash settlement for the loss. So, Ananda ended up with another Corvette exactly like the one that was stolen, and he was quite perplexed but accepted the situation, if not the car, as one of those things in life that happened and must be

accepted.

THE CAR AGAIN

Ananda again parked the car and
this time closer to the ashram which he
and his followers had established. The
replacement of his car happened during
winter time when storms could be fierce.
One night during an awful storm, a tree
fell over and crushed the car. Again,
because the car was so new, the
insurance company informed Ananda it
would be replaced. Ananda did not
understand how each time the car was
gone, although it was replaced by a

different car, essentially the same representation kept coming back to him.

One night Ananda prayed in complete sincerity, "Lord, I don't want this car but it keeps coming back to me. I do not understand because I have spent my life without material attachment. If it please the Lord, help me to understand why the car keeps returning to me so that this lesson can be understood by myself, your humble servant."

The response Ananda received was a voice he could hear throughout his room, "Ananda, haven't you read that we must let go of attachment as well as aversion? You must forsake your aversion."

Ananda was shocked by what he heard, and yet instantly realized it was true, and from then on, he embraced the Corvette. He learned about it, started driving it, and he became known as the yogi with a Corvette. He always told anyone who asked that it was just a car, and God wanted him to have it to overcome aversion.

As time passed Ananda became very used to his car and actually developed a liking, an attachment for it. He started driving it more often and became less self-conscious about it being a Corvette.

Then one day it happened. He was driving his car and absorbed in something other than what he was doing at that moment, and all of a sudden, he saw flashing lights behind him. He was being pulled over, and he did not know why. The police officer came up to his window and seeing the ochre-colored robe said, "so you are the yogi with the Corvette." The officer smiled and asked, "do you know why I pulled you over?"

At this point Ananda blushed and with all sincerity replied, "no."

The officer said, "the speed limit changed a little way back, but your speed did not. I am only going to give you a warning this time and ask that you pay attention to the speed limit signs. Have a good day, and by the way, it is a nice car."

The officer turned and walked back to his police cruiser. That incident was when Ananda knew it was time, he had overcome his aversion, and he sold the Corvette. With the money he received from selling the Corvette he bought a much more practical vehicle for delivering meals to help feed poor people and provide other services of the ashram. For a long time after the car was gone, many people asked Ananda about the Corvette. He smiled and replied simply that it was just one of life's lessons, and that he was glad to have had the opportunity to have the amazing sports car, even if for only a short time.

A while after having embraced the car, overcoming his aversion, and having sold the Corvette, Ananda was praying one evening in his room.

Suddenly a flash of light appeared and he found his guru, along with whom he intuitively recognized to be Baba, the guru of the mountains, both standing before him. He prostrated before Baba and before his guru, who lifted him, smiling. Ananda was happy to feel his guru's skin once again, and to have his guru before him in flesh and blood.

His guru told Ananda that he had overcome the obstacle for which he had come in this lifetime, his aversion was gone which meant his last challenge was gone, and with it the cycle of returning to earth for birth and death was over for him. His life would continue until his time to shed his body arrived. In the meantime, he would assume the name Satchidananda, which simply translated was the existence of expressed bliss. The removal of Dvesh was appropriate because it meant aversion, which he had overcome with the lesson of the Corvette.

Baba in turn embraced Ananda and told him he had earned the favor of God

and gave Ananda the keys to perform
the eight sacred abilities which signified
a fully self-realized yogi. These
included complete control over life and
death and over the material world. As
tears rolled down his face, Ananda
prostrated before him and thanked Baba.
Baba said that soon he would be able to
start to join his group, time permitting,
in the Himalayas, by travelling as he and
his guru did. Baba told him this would
help him transition to the spiritual world,
which he eventually would join forever

more, once he shed his physical body as his guru had done.

Ananda's guru then told him many other things about his life, the most important one being that Ananda remained happy throughout the rest of his life immersed in the Love of God, and reflecting the expression of that Divine Blissful state!

At that, Satchidananda's guru and Baba left him in another flash of light, and with a feeling so divine that whenever he recalled that sacred meeting, he would be flooded with the feelings of intense bliss that accompanied their visit.

Throughout his many remaining years Satchidananda shared his loving approach to life and the spiritual path with his many disciples, some of whom also became fully self realized. This was a reflection that Mikey fulfilled the purpose of existence, to truly understand life and share that understanding with

people devoted to their spiritual selves
and to God...

www.ingramcontent.com/pod-product-compliance
Lightning Source LLC
Chambersburg PA
CBHW022030170626
46808CB00003B/1122